For the Murray family,
with love from
J.A.

For Kate, George, Max and Tallullah,
and in memory of Charlie, with love.
T.H.

The author and publisher wish to thank
Martin Jenkins and the Philippine Department
of Tourism in London for their invaluable assistance
in the preparation of this book.

First published 1994 by Walker Books Ltd
87 Vauxhall Walk, London SE11 5HJ

This edition published 1998

2   4   6   8   10   9   7   5   3   1

Text © 1994 Judy Allen
Illustrations © 1994 Tudor Humphries

This book has been typeset in Times New Roman.

Printed in Hong Kong

British Library Cataloguing in Publication Data
A catalogue record for this book is available from the British Library.

ISBN 0-7445-6226-0

EAGLE

Written by
Judy Allen

Illustrated by
Tudor Humphries

WALKER BOOKS
AND SUBSIDIARIES
LONDON • BOSTON • SYDNEY

The eagle drifted above the forest canopy, broad wings resting on the upcurrents of air. The tops of the massive trees were only a few feet below him, and so close together that they looked like an uneven meadow.

The eagle was a powerful hunter, capable of astonishing bursts of speed, but he was lazy. He would do no more than cruise until he had sight of something worthy of his energies.

All the time he watched, with his pale eyes, eagle's eyes, eyes that see further and more clearly than those of any other creature on the planet.

His shadow moved beneath him, gliding across the heavy foliage. The animals of the forest roof became still and silent as it passed.

The trees thinned and parted and the dark silhouette slid across the ground: over the wide tracks made by the logging companies, and over the five human figures who walked near the edge of the forest where the clearings were wide and sunny.

The smallest of the humans, Miguel, flinched as the shadow touched him, and then glanced quickly around to see if anyone had noticed. No one had. The other three boys, and the teacher who was leading them, were staring up at the enormous bird as it circled slowly above them.

"*Haribon!*" said Mr Santos, using the Filipino name. "Very rare – very magnificent. Have any of you seen such a sight before?"

They had not. They were all from the city and only now were they old enough for the two-day forest trek.

At night they would stay safely at a nearby logging encampment, but even so it was an adventure, and those chosen to share it knew they were privileged.

Miguel, the youngest, was the only one who was not happy. He was constantly startled by the unfamiliar clickings, rustlings and sudden screeches of unseen forest animals. The towering trees and the confusion of tangled undergrowth made him feel small and scared. He tried hard to be as brave as the others, but the dense, damp forest seemed to him to be full of menace. Now, as the shadow of the massive bird of prey passed over him a second time, and then a third, it began to seem like the spirit of the forest itself – warning him, threatening him.

While the others gathered to admire the rich patterns on a reticulated python looped elegantly around a branch, he watched the patch of sky above, hoping the eagle would not return a fourth time.

The sky remained empty. The bird was no longer near the clearing, he was standing on a branch more than thirty metres up a hardwood tree. He had caught nothing to bring back to the female who waited on the nest beside him. She would not hunt for some weeks yet. She would not leave the two-month-old eaglet she had hatched on the vast tough-leaved fern that grew near the crown of the tree.

The eaglet opened its beak and yawned with hunger. The male shifted on his perch.

Miguel followed as Mr Santos led the group to a twisted tree that grew half-wrapped around its neighbour. The figs that clustered on its branches were just beginning to ripen.

"If we get out of sight," said the teacher, "and stay quiet, we'll see what comes to feed."

They waited, brushing scurrying ants off their legs and insects from their arms. They waited until their heads swam with the steamy green smell of jungle.

A hornbill came first, tearing at the tree with its great beak, then throwing back its head to roll the fruit down its throat. It was joined by two more, and soon a distant chittering sound told them that macaque monkeys were near.

Miguel glanced upwards, hoping to see them.

High on a branch at the edge of the clearing the eagle sat, unmoving, its shape clearly outlined against the sky.

Miguel's shout sent the hornbills clattering into the distance.

"What's the matter?" said Mr Santos, looking around, looking up. "The eagle?"

"It's watching me!" said Miguel.

"It's watching," said Mr Santos, "but it isn't watching you." He held up his hand to quieten the others. "It's hunting for flying lemurs or flying squirrels."

"Why doesn't it hunt somewhere else?" said Miguel, dizzy with staring upwards.

"The loggers have worked all around here," said Mr Santos, "cutting the trees and taking them. They have turned this patch of forest into an island. The *haribon* is a forest bird, and cannot hunt anywhere else. It must patrol continually in order to survive."

The eagle spread his wings and flapped slowly and heavily out of sight.

"There, it's gone!" said Mr Santos.

"It'll come back," said Miguel. "It's after me!"

"You're frightened of the jungle because it's unknown territory," said Mr Santos, "but I'm with you, and I know the dangers. There is no danger from the eagle."

"I can't help it," said Miguel. "I don't like it."

"Listen," said Mr Santos. "There are two kinds of fear – fear of true danger which is useful because it makes you protect yourself, and fear of fear itself, which is not useful. What is worse, if you do nothing about it, it can spoil your life. Do you understand?"

"Yes," said Miguel.

"The bird startled you because it appeared suddenly, that's all. You must let go of this fear."

He had been speaking softly, and the hornbills were beginning to return to the figs.

Mr Santos pointed towards them. "Don't spoil all this for yourself," he said.

"OK," said Miguel.

"Are you all right now?" said Mr Santos.

"Yes," said Miguel. But he wasn't.

The leader of the macaque monkeys appeared, clinging
to a rope of liana, drawn by the scent of the ripe figs,
but wary of the humans. The rest of the troop was
high out of sight, rustling and chattering overhead.

With a suddenness that made everyone jump,
pandemonium broke out in the tops of the trees.
Something went crashing through the topmost
branches like a powerful wind, the macaques
shrieked, their leader ran howling up the
liana-rope and vanished among the branches.
A violent chase took place, invisible above
the glossy foliage, and then stopped abruptly.
In the silence a few torn leaves floated down,
into a clearing that was now empty of forest life.

"You know what that was!" said Mr Santos.

They did, they had guessed. "The eagle!" said one.
"Did it get a monkey?" said the second. "It sounded
like a monster!" said the third. Miguel said nothing.
His eyes glittered and he was shaking all over.

Mr Santos rested his hand lightly on Miguel's
shoulder. "The monkey may have escaped," he said.
"But we have to be realistic – the eagle needs to eat."

Miguel shook his head. He was too shocked to speak.

"He thinks it's haunting him," said one of the other boys, not unkindly. "It's bewitched him," said another.

"He has bewitched himself," said Mr Santos. "All right, Miguel, I will help you break the spell." He walked a short distance away and picked up a long stick. Then he returned and scuffed a clear patch on the ground with one foot. He handed the stick to Miguel. "Now," he said, "draw the eagle."

Miguel looked at him.

"Draw it," ordered Mr Santos. "Here, on the ground."

Everyone waited.

Miguel took the stick and stared down at the earth. Then he began to draw the predatory shadow of the bird, exactly the way it had first fallen on him. He drew the enormous outline, the powerful wings, the strong body, the head to one side so the heavy beak showed.

He drew well, and when he had finished no one could possibly have been in any doubt about what the picture showed.

"Good," said Mr Santos.

"Look carefully at your picture.

That is not the eagle you have drawn – that is your fear. Now, cross it out!"

Miguel stared at the earth-drawing for a moment. Then he grasped the stick in both hands, stabbed one end of it into the earth near the head, and crossed out the image in a single sweeping movement, from the head, through one wing, in a curve across the body, and out beyond the tail.

He stood back and threw down the stick.

"Excellent," said Mr Santos. "The eagle itself is free, but your fear is destroyed."

The others gathered around, impressed, to have a closer look at the pattern on the ground.

"You see!" said Mr Santos to Miguel. "You're all right now, aren't you?"

"Yes," said Miguel obediently. But he wasn't.

J 131, 466

That night in his dreams, his fear hovered above him.
Next day, as they left the logging camp and walked
back through the forest, it hung over him like a cloud.
A stone worked its way into his shoe and he knelt
and tugged at the laces. The others moved on,

unaware they were leaving him behind. Not wanting to
cause another disturbance by calling them, Miguel
tried to deal quickly with the stone – dragging
off his shoe, shaking it, forcing his foot
back into the warm, damp lining.

Something dropped from the sky above him with the speed of a falling stone, cutting out the sunlight so that for a second he was in a tiny pool of night. Something living and warm and heavy struck his shoulder and knocked him off balance. Coarse feathers brushed his skin. As he rolled on his back, beating wings filled his vision.

From where he lay, Miguel saw the eagle surging upwards again, and he understood why it had plunged to earth – in its talons it carried the long body and hooded head of a king cobra. He heard running footsteps, he was aware of Mr Santos at his side, but he could not look away.

The thin, dark length of the snake was still twitching, though its head had been crushed. It looped from the eagle's claws in a sweeping S-shape, exactly matching the line he had scored through the earth-drawing.

Mr Santos pulled Miguel to his feet, his face serious.

"It's as well he wasn't as afraid of you as you are of him," he said. "The cobra is deadly."

On the immense fern nest, high in the hardwood tree, the adult birds tore at the dead snake and fed the gaping-mouthed eaglet.

On the ground, no more than a foot from the spot where it had been taken, the other boys thumped Miguel on the back and told him he was a hero.

He looked up at Mr Santos. "He knocked me out of the way," he said, "he knocked me away from the snake."

"I'm afraid he was only interested in catching a meal," said Mr Santos.

"I know that!" said Miguel. "I mean – he *touched* me – and I'm not frightened now!"

"So are you all right at last?" said Mr Santos, dusting him down.

"Yes," said Miguel, laughing. "Yes, I am." And he was.

EAGLE FACT SHEET

THE PHILIPPINE EAGLE is possibly the biggest eagle in the world, and certainly one of the rarest. There may be fewer than 250 of them, living in forests on four islands in the Philippines Archipelago, in the western Pacific Ocean. Less than a century ago there were over 1,000 Philippine eagles on one of these islands alone.

Although often called the monkey-eating eagle, it actually feeds on many other animals as well, including flying lemurs, rats, hornbills, snakes, and even young deer.

◆ WHAT ARE THE DANGERS FOR EAGLES? ◆

At one time the main threat was that Philippine eagles were hunted — for sport, and because people believed they took livestock. Nowadays, although some hunting still goes on, the most serious threat is the destruction of the forests on which the eagles depend for food and nesting sites. The trees are cut down by logging companies for timber, and by local people to clear space for crops.

◆ IS ANYONE HELPING PHILIPPINE EAGLES? ◆

Yes. In 1969, the Philippine government set up the Philippine Eagle Conservation Programme, with the help of WWF (World Wide Fund for Nature) and several other conservation organizations, including the local Haribon Foundation based in the Philippine capital, Manila. At the same time, it was made illegal to harm the eagle or its nesting areas. Projects to try to conserve the eagle have continued ever since.

◆ ARE EFFORTS TO SAVE EAGLES SUCCEEDING? ◆

It is difficult to say. Although many more people in the Philippines now know about their eagle and would like it to be protected, the forest continues to be cut down. Unfortunately, the government does not have either the money or trained people to stop the destruction — even when it takes place in a national park or game reserve.

◆ IS THERE ANYTHING YOU CAN DO? ◆

Yes. You can join the junior section of WWF, or persuade your family or your school to join.

WWF
Panda House
Weyside Park
Godalming
GU7 1XR
United Kingdom